GLOWKELP FOREST

UNDYING CAVES

MERROW RUINS

THE FORBIDDEN CITY

CAVERNS OF MADNESS

RIMOROSA'S LAIR

this book belongs to:

_____

For quiet, unsung heroes around the world. —B.H.

STERLING CHILDREN'S BOOKS
New York

An Imprint of Sterling Publishing Co., Inc.
1166 Avenue of the Americas
New York, NY 10036

ISBN: 978-1-4549-2161-5

Distributed in Canada by Sterling Publishing Co., Inc.
c/o Canadian Manda Group, 664 Annette Street
Toronto, Ontario, Canada M6S 2C8
Distributed in the United Kingdom by GMC Distribution Services
Castle Place, 166 High Street, Lewes, East Sussex, England BN7 1XU

For information about custom editions, special sales, and premium and corporate purchases,
please contact Sterling Special Sales at 800-805-5489 or specialsales@sterlingpublishing.com.

Manufactured in China
Lot #:
2 4 6 8 10 9 7 5 3 1
07/16

www.sterlingpublishing.com

Text by Brian Hastings
Illustrations by Tony Mora and Alexis Seabrook
Art direction by Jo Obarowski
Design by Irene Vandervoort

MERRYN'S JOURNEY

BRIAN HASTINGS

with illustrations by

Tony Mora and Alexis Seabrook

STERLING CHILDREN'S BOOKS
New York

In a little cottage, where the cliffs meet the waves, lived a young girl named Merryn.

Each day while her father went out to sea to catch fish, Merryn tended her garden and tinkered in her work shed. She loved to build new tools for her dad: a spyglass, a lobster trap, and even a two-way radio. Each night Merryn waited at the edge of the cliffs, excited to show him what she had made that day.

Sometimes the winds were strong and her father didn't catch any fish. On those days, they didn't have a lot to eat. But Merryn knew that whatever happened, her father would always protect her.

"Sing me a lullaby?" Merryn asked one night as she climbed into bed. Her father closed his eyes for a moment, thinking. Then he sang a song about a beautiful, mysterious world that lay below the sea.

He sang of ravenous leviathan serpents that guarded an ancient, secret realm . . . of graceful, brave merrows who were part fish and part human . . . of a mysterious undersea tower that shone lights up toward ships from below . . . and of a giant, deadly beast that pulled those ships to the bottom of the sea. And finally, he sang of a vast and beautiful sunken city made entirely of gold, where all the riches from the ships were kept.

Merryn didn't believe in such things, of course, but she always loved to hear her father's stories. She fell asleep, happily imagining a world of undiscovered wonders that lay hidden beneath the rolling waves.

And then, the next night, Merryn's world changed forever.

Her father didn't return from the sea.

She waited at the edge of the cliffs, holding up a candle to guide him home.

She watched for his boat all through the night, but it never appeared.

At last, she fell asleep at the edge of the cliffs. As she slept, she had a dream. A dream so vivid and real, she was sure it must be true.

She saw her father trapped at the bottom of the sea.

And she was the only one who could help him.

When she woke up, she knew what she had to do.

Merryn went to the shore and got to work. She sifted through the scraps of metal and wood her father had caught in his nets, pulling out pieces she thought she could use. One by one, she hammered the pieces together, until she had built a tiny, rickety submarine.

She dragged it to the shore, squeezed inside, and dove down beneath the waves to search for her father.

But the world below was filled with surprises.
Forests of lantern jellies lit up the sea like a thousand stars in the sky. Shadows of giant, undulating serpents loomed in the distance.

As Merryn sailed through a dark winding cavern, she froze in fear. Right in front of her, a giant sea spider slept in its web! Merryn tried to sneak by without waking the spider, but then she noticed a wriggling cocoon caught in the web. She couldn't leave whatever was trapped inside. Swallowing her fear, she swam toward it to help.

She opened the cocoon, and a playful baby serpent quickly glided away from the sleeping spider.

Merryn took back off on her journey, and the odd little creature followed her, swishing his tail to get her attention.

Eventually she gave in and waved back to him. She decided to call him Swish.

Swish led Merryn to a hidden nook within the cave, where she found an old diving suit and a strange striped shell called a zephyr whelk that her father had described in his lullabies. Her father said that ancient sea explorers had used them to breathe underwater. Merryn put the shell to her lips and felt a rush of air bubbles fill her cheeks.

With a mix of excitement and fear, Merryn wondered if all her father's songs were real.

Swish and Merryn dove deeper. They discovered the shimmering ruins of an ancient village.

Merryn's eyes widened in awe. Swimming amidst the jagged stone walls was a merrow maiden. They were real after all!

The merrow knew Merryn was looking for her father. She explained that there was a great tower beneath the sea called the Deeplight that lured ships to their demises. Her father's boat might have been among them.

Merryn thanked the merrow and quickly set off with Swish in search of the ominous tower.

They discovered a graveyard of sunken ships that spanned miles and miles, and at its center was the Deeplight.

Merryn froze as she saw a giant, tentacled creature swimming high above her. It followed the lights of the tower, looking for any sign of movement. She and Swish remained completely still.

When the great beast had passed, they searched through the wreckage. At last, Merryn saw her father's boat!

But it was cracked in two, and her father was nowhere to be seen. Only his journal was left inside, in a pocket of air inside the cabin.

In a rage, Merryn attacked the tower, ramming into its lights with her submarine until they shattered and went dark.

She had destroyed the Deeplight. Never again would any ship fall prey to it.

Merryn drifted down to the sea floor. She opened her father's journal and read the final entry:

I fear I may not make it back. The creature that pulled me down still circles outside the boat, waiting. I wish I was home to protect Merryn. I must try to return to the surface. There is an old diving bell not far away . . . If only I can elude that beast.

Merryn sat staring at the journal. There had been no diving bell near the boat, but she was determined to find it.

She looked up to see Swish beckoning to her anxiously. He led her to a beautiful coral garden, where the merrow maiden was lying on a bed of rock. She was hurt! Merryn bandaged her wounds with strands of kelp, then foraged for scallops for her to eat. Slowly the merrow began to regain her strength.

She said she had been attacked by the same creature Merryn saw at the Deeplight. The great beast was known as the Rimorosa, and it lived below a sunken city made of gold.

"If your father has been captured, he may be trapped within its golden halls," the merrow said.

Merryn thought of her father and the diving bell. Did the Rimorosa capture him after he made it inside? She set out in search of the city, leaving Swish behind to help protect the merrow.

Merryn followed the merrow's directions to the lost city of gold. It was the most beautiful place she had ever seen. There were more riches there than she could have imagined, but the city was completely empty. There was no sign of her dad.

And Merryn felt more alone than ever.

With her last ounce of hope, she sailed down out of the city to continue her search.

And there, in the dark waters below, she saw her father! He was inside a diving bell, just as he had written.

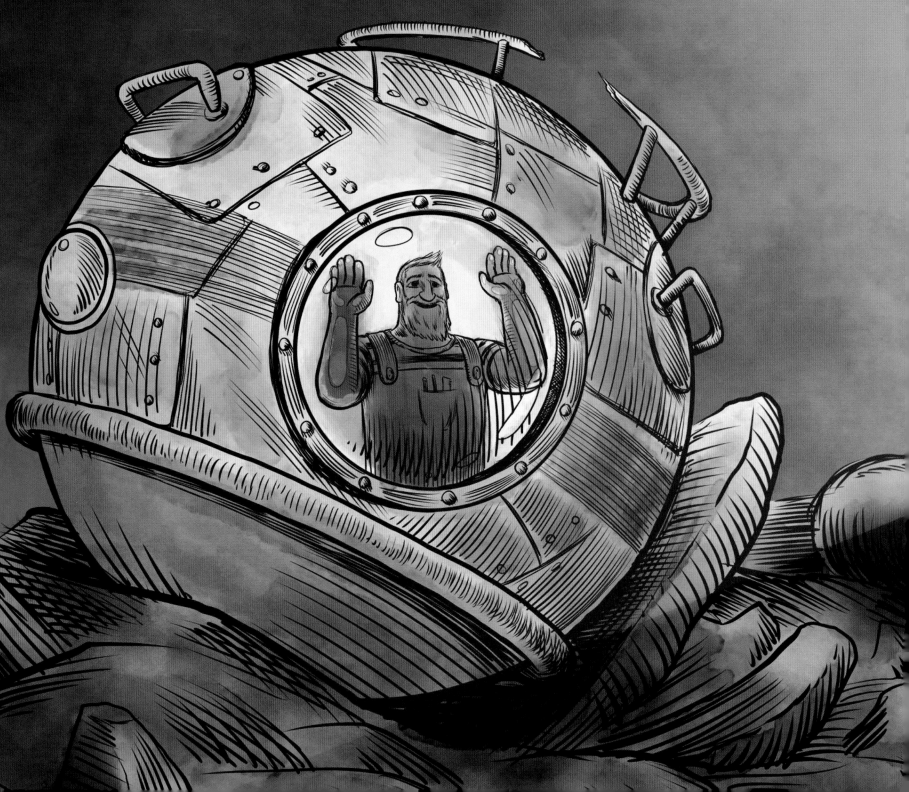

Just when Merryn reached him, a great red tentacle grabbed hold of her, squeezing her so tightly she couldn't move. She looked with horror into the yellow eyes of the Rimorosa.

But as she wriggled to get free, a terrifying roar echoed from above. She looked up to see the giant, toothy maw of a queen leviathan coming straight toward her! She closed her eyes in fear. The water shook and she heard an awful crunch as the creature's jaws slammed shut.

But when Merryn opened her eyes, she was unhurt. The leviathan had pulled her and her father away from the grasping arms of the terrible Rimorosa.

Merryn saw Swish wagging his tail next to her.

The queen leviathan was his mother! She had saved Merryn in return for Merryn saving Swish.

Merryn and her father held onto the tails of the serpents and together they rose up out of the depths. The Rimorosa's thrashing tentacles cracked the foundations of the golden city, causing it to collapse on top of the beast.

Safely back at home, Merryn and her father said good-bye to the serpents. Merryn promised to come play with Swish each day in the deep waters below the cliffs.

As she helped her father build a new boat, they told each other about all the strange and beautiful things they had seen.

Now, each day, Merryn and her father go out to sea together. The fish have become plentiful again. And Merryn wonders, as she looks out over the waves, what other mysteries might lurk below. "Someday," she says to herself, smiling, "someday, I'll find out."

A NOTE FROM THE AUTHOR

The initial idea for MERRYN'S JOURNEY came about because I wanted to create a hero for my daughter to look up to. I had noticed that when she told me about the female characters she liked in movies, she would almost always start by saying how pretty they were. Being pretty had even become a big part of her own identity. She tended to receive more compliments on her appearance than for being artistic, kind, funny, smart, or hardworking. I wanted to make a story for her where the main character was heroic and memorable only because of her inner qualities. And that's how Merryn first came to be.

At Insomniac Games we've been creating worlds and characters for 21 years, and each one has been a labor of love, but making the game SONG OF THE DEEP was a special journey for us. The art of this world has a haunting and beautiful feel to it—it really transports you to another place. The illustrations in this book, by Tony Mora and Alexis Seabrook, capture that feeling, and the loneliness, resilience, and unfailing hope that are core to the story. Merryn is a character we have come to love over the course of creating the game and the book, and the scenes here represent the essence of what makes her heroic and inspiring to us.

Working on this story was an incredible experience. It forced me to think about the things I value most and the kind of person I want to be. Merryn is a character I didn't want to say good-bye to. I hope her journey is one that you enjoy and remember as well.

—BRIAN HASTINGS